VINE STREET MYSTERIES

BOOK 1
THE KITTEN WHO SAVED CHRISTMAS

To Matlock girls,

Always Believe!

NOVA DUDUIS

Printed in the United States of America
ISBN: 978-1-956019-31-5 (hardcover)
ISBN: 978-1-956019-32-2 (paperback)
ISBN: 978-1-956019-33-9 (ebook)

Library of Congress Control Number: 2021921977

**Canoe Tree
Press**

4697 Main Street
Manchester Center, VT 05255
Canoe Tree Press is a division of DartFrog Books

Dedicated to Farrah, the sweetest one of them all.

1. Pearl's house

3. Pearly White Dentistry

2. Little Paws Clinic

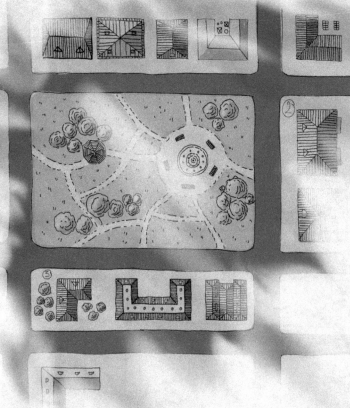

CHAPTER ONE

CHRISTMAS EVE

"Ginni, honey, why don't you open your last present?" asked Dad.

Another Christmas Eve at the Pearl home was almost over. We'd attended candlelight services, eaten our usual delicious steak dinner, all but one of the gifts had been opened and enjoyed, and the fire in the fireplace had just about burned itself out.

My younger brother's last gift was a brand new Huffy Valcon 6-speed bike. I had noticed Frankie eyeing it at Handyman's Hardware Store for months. Every Christmas, we each receive a 'special' gift to be opened last.

I eyed my 'special' gift and sighed. This was it: my last gift on the first Christmas without Mom. Even at only ten years old, I knew Dad was trying his best to hold it together—to hold us together—and to keep the family's Christmas traditions. Mom's death had hit us hard. How could it not?

And it had been so unexpected. Mom was a fighter pilot—or at least she was until she died when her plane was shot down. Mom was the heart and soul of our family. Christmas had been her favorite holiday; celebrating it without her just seemed wrong. But we carried on anyway. It was what she would have wanted us to do.

Shifting on the couch, I leaned forward to pick up the pretty yellow package tied with a red bow. My hair fell onto my face as I leaned forward. Everyone loves my long red hair, but without Mom's help, I have a hard time managing it. Now I usually just wear it in a ponytail.

Just as I was reaching for my 'special' gift, all the lights went off.

"That's strange," puzzled Dad. "It's snowing, but not hard enough to affect the electricity."

Frankie ran to the window and looked up and down Vine Street. My brother is three years younger than I. He is an average-sized seven-year-old with brown hair and blue eyes. Frankie has freckles sprinkled across his nose, while I have freckles all over my face. Mom always called them angel kisses. Guess I was kissed a lot!

"The lights are on at the Pebbles' house next door. Even Stanley's house has lights on," Frankie reported. "The power never went out like this when Mom was alive."

While we all missed Mom, Frankie's heart had suffered the biggest break. He and Mom had been very close, and Frankie has such a tender heart. Sometimes I wonder if I'd ever hear him laugh again.

As soon as Frankie had made his announcement that the neighbors had power, our lights came on.

"Oh, well," laughed Dad. "Now you can see to open your last present, Ginni."

Dad and I had just settled back onto the couch when off went the lights again. This time, even though Frankie was still by the front door, he didn't have time to check the neighborhood before they came back on. Then the lights went off, on, off, and on again—way too many times to count!

"Frankie, are you messing with the light switch?" I scolded.

Frankie turned to me with hurt in his eyes and said, "I swear, I'm not touching it!"

I felt a little bad I had accused him, but this was just too strange.

Dad, being a dentist, is a very scientific guy. He has a dental clinic downtown called Pearly White Dentistry. Now it was time for him to investigate. "Perhaps I should check the fuse box," he said as he lifted himself off the couch.

He didn't even get past the piano before Alexa turned on—by herself—and played a holiday favorite, "White Christmas."

In total awe, the three of us stared at each other. This wasn't just any holiday song. It was Mom's favorite Christmas melody. She used to play it on the piano over and over all throughout December.

Since the lights stayed on and Bing Crosby was still crooning "White Christmas," we forgot all about checking the fuse box.

None of us moved throughout the first verse of the song. Tears streamed down Frankie's cheeks, but I was too spooked to cry. What was going on?

Suddenly I heard a tremendous swooshing noise outside. Dad and Frankie were looking around, confused. I guessed they had heard it, too.

"What was that?" I asked.

We all rushed to the window. A huge barn owl was circling around and around the house.

Then we heard a tap, tap, tap and then more swooshing sounds as the big owl flew faster and faster around the house.

"Dad, I'm scared," said Frankie.

"I'm sure it's nothing," Dad said. "Don't worry, you two; I'll get to the bottom of this."

When Dad opened the inside door, I saw the owl knocking on the storm door with its beak. What in the world was it doing?

Dad then opened the storm door and took a step forward, and the owl took flight. It circled the house again, then settled on a branch of the maple tree in our front yard.

As soon as Dad had opened the door, a gust of wind blew into the house; boy, was it cold outside. I shivered and wondered, as I often did, just how animals can live outside during our cold northern winters.

"How strange," Dad said. "*Tyto furcatas* don't usually fly so close to houses. I wonder what's gotten into that one."

I shook my head and said, "Dad, must you always use the scientific names for things? Isn't it a barn owl?"

"Well, yes, Ginni, it is," said Dad with a wide grin, "but I endeavor to be accurate."

"Okay, I'm going to call him Tyto, then. I wonder if he's just cold."

"I do know one thing," Dad said. "Whatever's going on, this is definitely our strangest Christmas ever."

Before I could comment, Tyto let out a hoot, then another one. With wide eyes, he looked down at us.

"I think he's trying to tell us something," I said.

I leaned forward, almost getting knocked over by Frankie. He pushed past me and dashed out into the snow.

Dad shouted, "Frankie, come back! You don't even have your slippers on!" But nothing was stopping Frankie.

At the base of our maple tree sat a bundle of fur.

It was the cutest black kitten ever!

"Wait!" yelled Dad. "You don't know if that kitten is friendly!"

Too late; Frankie already had it in his arms, and it was nuzzling his neck. It took Dad and me a few seconds to catch up to Frankie.

"We've gotta take it into the house to warm up, Dad," cried Frankie. I knew Dad could not say no to Frankie's pleading eyes.

Dad nodded. "Okay, bring it in . . . for now!"

As the three of us were hurrying back to the house, I glanced back at the majestic owl perched in the tree. There sat Tyto, grinning at us.

While Frankie held the black kitten, Dad looked it over, pronounced it to be a girl, and proclaimed that she looked safe and healthy enough to stay the night. I was so relieved!

Then I spotted a little tag caught under her purple collar. I carefully reached over and pulled it out.

"It's a name tag," I reported. "Her name is Neelia." Just as I said that Neelia licked my hand and purred. We all laughed.

"Who's up for a cup of hot cocoa while the three of you settle in and Ginni opens her last present?" Dad asked.

No one in our house would ever turn down a cup of Dad's hot cocoa. He makes the best hot cocoa ever! Frankie and I were sitting on the couch with Neelia between us when Dad brought in the hot chocolate.

"Three hot cocoas and one saucer of warm milk," Dad announced.

Tears started welling up in my brown eyes as I watched Dad place the saucer of warm milk on the floor for Neelia. Dad had been doing all he could since Mom died to help keep us emotionally together by staying cheerful, but sometimes it seemed as if he were faking it. When he put down the saucer, there was a genuine smile on his face. It was the first moment since we'd received the news about Mom that a small part of grief lifted from my heart and was replaced with love: love for Mom, Dad, Frankie, and now Neelia.

Dad reached down and placed my last present in my lap. I was glad to have the distraction so I wouldn't cry in front of him and Frankie. I leaned down toward the present, looking it over carefully, mostly to hide my face until I could compose myself.

By the time I got a good look at the present, I was intrigued. It was heavy, and I could think of only one thing it could be: a sewing machine. Mom had just started letting me use her sophisticated sewing machine, and I'd loved learning from her. She'd tease me by hinting that I would need one of my own someday. But how could this be? Mom died way before anyone would have thought to go Christmas shopping. And if this *weren't* a sewing machine, how could I hide my disappointment? My emotions were on a roller coaster.

I finally started tearing off the yellow wrapping paper, and there it was, a Brother Computerized Sewing Machine For Beginners. I could no longer hold back my tears.

"But—how?" I managed to squeak out.

"Your mom and I went shopping for this just a couple of days before she was deployed," Dad told me. "She was so excited to buy you your first sewing machine and was happy to see you taking after her with your love of crafts. It's been hiding under my bed since this summer. It's the last gift she ever bought, and I'm pleased that it's a sewing machine for you.

"I'll be saving your mom's fancy machine so you can take it over when you're older and you're ready. But for now, you can keep yourself busy learning on your new Brother machine. I can't wait to see what you'll create!"

I raced into Dad's arms, and Frankie joined us in a family hug—all of us with tears. But for the first time since Mom died, all of us were crying not from grief but from love.

When we broke from the hug, Dad took the saucer and the cocoa mugs back to the kitchen while I dug into the box that held my sewing machine. That's when I heard Frankie's musical laugh. I hadn't heard that sound in months. I looked up, and there he was, playing tug-of-war with Neelia over his shoestring. I saw Dad step back into the living room, and the two of us shared a look. We both were so happy to hear Frankie laugh again.

There could never be another Christmas as unique nor as mysterious as this one, I thought.

CHAPTER TWO

CHRISTMAS DAY

The next morning, I woke early and headed downstairs to find Dad in his home office. As magical as Christmas Eve had been, I now was really worried about whether or not we could keep Neelia.

We live in my grandparents' old house—my mom's parents' home. They got tired of the northern winters, so when they moved to Florida, we took over their house. I love it! While it is small, it is unique. There is a curved stairway leading from the upstairs bedrooms to the living room and another curved staircase that leads from the kitchen to the basement. Mom used to catch us sliding on our bottoms, going bumpity-bump down the stairs, but neither Frankie nor I had done that since she died. In addition to the curved staircases, there are curved shelving units on either side of the fireplace and curved built-in bookshelves in the dining room and bedrooms. Lots of character, my mom used to say—and I agree.

"Dad," I said, "you know Frankie really needs Neelia right now. Do you see how the two of them get along? It's very special. You have to let him keep her." Dad lowered his head, but before he could speak, I continued, "I had a much better speech in my head while I was upstairs in my bedroom, but I can't come up with all the words now." And neither could I go on with my speech because tears were beginning to well up in my eyes. But I did manage to squeak out, "He already loves her."

It was right after my botched speech that Frankie came down the stairs, going bumpity-bump with Neelia bouncing in his lap.

Dad looked up at me again, and now tears were streaming down my cheeks. What a difference this new friend was already making! Frankie finally felt happy enough for a bumpity-bump stair ride.

"Can we keep her? Can we, huh?" pleaded Frankie as he walked into Dad's office carrying Neelia.

"The two of you are ganging up on me," laughed Dad. "It's too early to tell. It's Christmas Day, and the vet's office is closed. I'll call first thing tomorrow and make an appointment. Maybe she has a microchip. She's such a sweet little kitten, and she has a name tag. I can't imagine she doesn't belong to someone. But we'll see. Meanwhile, let's take some good pictures of her and make some 'Found: Kitten' signs you can post on Main Street," Dad suggested.

"Do we have to?" Frankie whispered.

"Come now, Son, if you had lost your kitten, you'd want her returned, wouldn't you?"

"Yes, but she already feels like my kitten," protested Frankie.

At that moment, Neelia jumped down from Frankie's arms and started curling herself around Dad's ankles. Then she pawed at his legs until Dad reached down and lifted her onto his lap. I had to turn my face so Dad wouldn't see my big grin. Dad was acting tough, but I could tell he was falling for Neelia's charms just as much as Frankie and I were.

"I know this is going to be hard, but we are still going to do everything we can to make sure some boy or girl isn't crying their heart out missing her," Dad said. "But life is full of surprises, Frankie; don't lose hope."

Dad reached for his phone on the corner of his desk and handed it to Frankie. "Here's my phone. Now, you and your sister go take some cute pictures, and I'll work on a message for the sign—after I find your mom's Air Force wings I was going to take to the jeweler for repair. I was holding them just before you guys came in!"

"You know, Dad," I teased, "if I had my own cell phone, you wouldn't have to be without yours." I had been bringing up a need for my own cell phone for months now. But I knew better than to beg. By now, it had become a running joke between Dad and me.

"Scat, the three of you!" Dad teased back as he started looking under his desk for the wings. "And I expect some quality pictures!" he called after us as we left his office.

It was easy taking pictures; Neelia seemed to pose for the camera. We took pictures of her under the Christmas tree, sitting on the couch like a princess, and playing with Frankie's shoelace.

When we were done, I took Dad's phone back to him. After he had printed the best photos, Frankie and I set out to make the signs.

I started the project by running downstairs to our little craft room in the basement. We had a desk there and some storage bins full of supplies. Mom, Frankie, and I liked creating things, and we were always trying our hands at various crafts. I paused a moment and looked at some of our previous projects on display around the room. I sighed as I grabbed markers, colored pencils and pens, crayons, rulers, and scissors and headed back upstairs. Then Frankie and I got busy right away creating the signs.

"You thirsty?" I asked after several minutes. When Frankie nodded, I went to the kitchen to grab a couple of juice boxes for us. When I came back, I could tell Frankie was hiding something with his hand.

"What's that?" I asked, looking down at the stack of papers on Frankie's workstation.

"Nothin'," Frankie said coyly.

"I can see a crayon drawing you're trying to hide under that stack of paper, Frankie. Show me," I said.

Frankie shyly pulled out the drawing he had done. It was a crazy, mean-looking cat with the headline 'Are You Missing A Cat That Bites?' After laughing, I was about to scold him when he said, "Just joking!"

In about an hour, we had twenty signs completed. The pictures of Neelia printed out perfectly. We wrote 'Found: Kitten' at the top and put our name and phone number at the bottom so someone could call and claim her. After that, we added a few drawings of paw prints, cat faces, etc., around the borders.

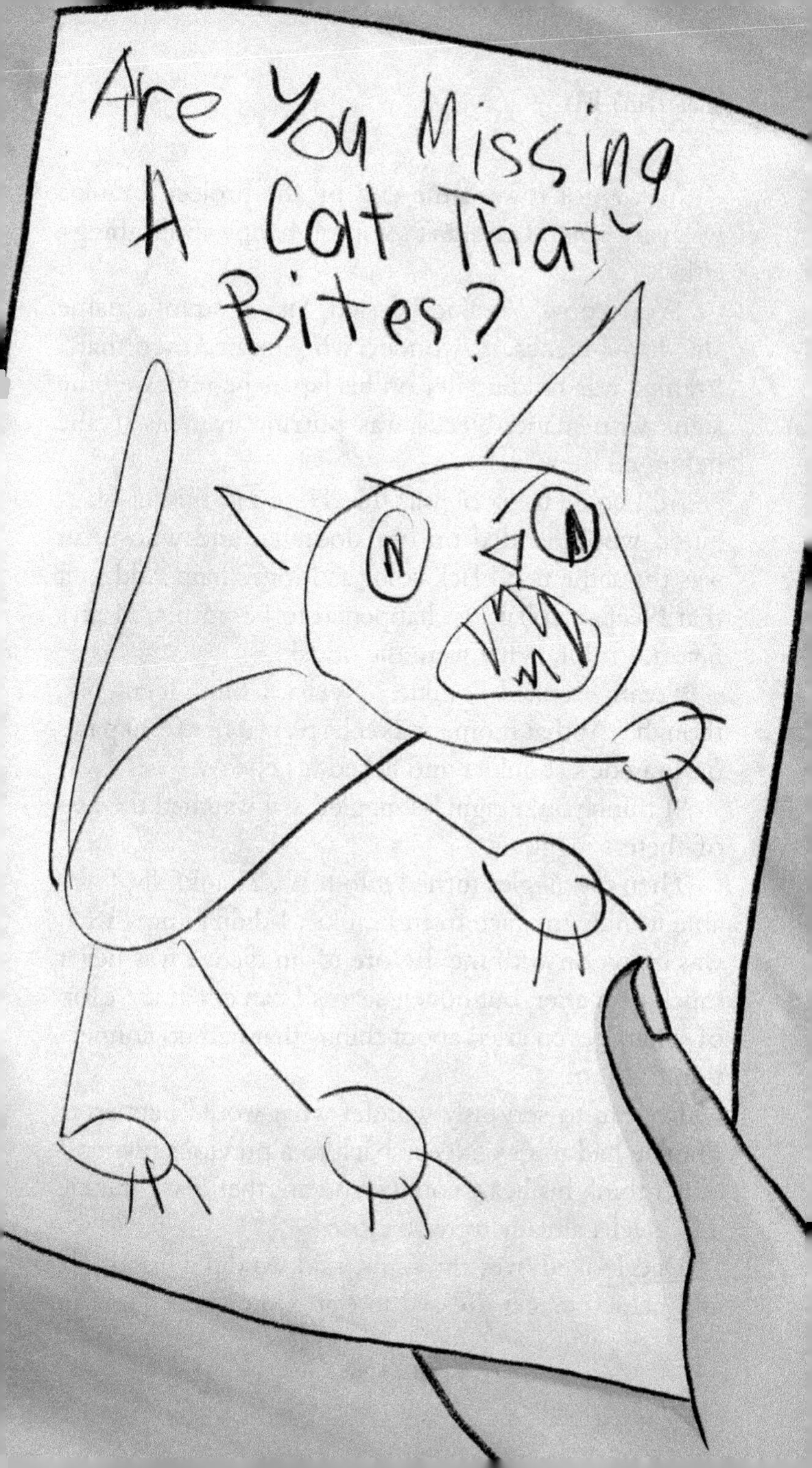
Are You Missing
A Cat That
Bites?

As we got toward the end of the project, Frankie was very quiet. I couldn't say I felt happy about things, either.

"You know, Frankie," I said, "it's a strange name she has—Neelia. I wonder who named her that." Frankie was holding her on his lap as he reviewed the signs we'd made. Neelia was purring away as if she belonged there.

All I could think of was this: Here was this jet-black kitten who'd landed on our doorstep and whose fur was the same rich black color as Mom's hair. Add to it that Neelia's collar just happened to be purple, Mom's favorite color. What were the odds?

"Yeah," replied Frankie. "Neelia. I think it fits her, though." At that moment, Neelia placed her front paws on Frankie's shoulder and licked his cheek.

"I think you're right," I giggled as I watched the two of them snuggle.

Then my giggles turned into tears. Thankfully, I was able to hide my face from Frankie. I didn't know what was going on with me. Before Mom died, I was never much of a crier, but now it seems I can cry at the drop of a hat. I even cried about things that had no connection to Mom.

I began to seriously wonder what would happen if Frankie had to give Neelia back to a previous owner. I didn't think his heart could stand another loss. Frankie and Neelia already were so close.

Dad looked over the signs, said we did a good job, and helped us get dressed in our winter gear. He also gave us a bag for carrying the signs, tape, and twine so that Frankie and I could hang up the notices downtown.

From our house, the walk downtown takes only a few minutes. That's the nice thing about living in Makawee. I've always thought Makawee is a cool name for a town. It's the Sioux word for 'mothering,' and the town takes pride in caring for its citizens. Makawee is big enough to have most everything you need, yet small enough that you can walk downtown from almost anywhere.

And we have a pretty downtown. A couple blocks of businesses are circled around Central Park. Central Park is a cool place. On Thursday nights during spring, summer, and fall, it houses a huge Farmers' Market. It seems everyone comes out for it—not only to buy cucumbers and tomatoes but simply to hang out. And except in the month of July, the high school band plays in the gazebo, which brings out even more families. I can't wait until I get to be up there on stage playing the clarinet. At least, that's the instrument I plan on playing in the band. Mom played the clarinet, and she'd been anxious to start giving me some lessons. I don't know if I'll ever be good enough to sit first chair like she did, but I'm looking forward to giving it a try.

Frankie and I passed by the gazebo on our way to hang our first sign, and I closed my eyes and saw myself sitting with the high school band holding my shining clarinet. In my daydream, I was surrounded by many of my friends who were also band members, and we were all playing for a large audience sitting in folding chairs and on blankets spread across the lawn.

I stopped daydreaming when my mind's eye saw Dad and Frankie sitting in the audience, along with an empty chair where Mom should have been.

Both Frankie and I were melancholy as we started our mission. This being Christmas Day, all the shoppers were gone, and the businesses were closed. Downtown was deserted; it felt odd to be the only ones walking around. We placed the signs on trees, light poles, and store windows.

With each sign we taped up, I said a little prayer asking that Neelia's owner would not see it. But who was I kidding? Such a sweet, adorable kitten—with a name tag—had to belong to someone close by, didn't she?

Frankie was quiet as we put up the signs. When we were done, we headed back home. Frankie kept wanting me to assure him no one would claim Neelia.

There are times when I really miss Mom, and this was one of them. She always knew the right things to say. She could talk to Frankie and make him feel better no matter what was bothering him, and Frankie always confided in Mom. While people say I look just like her (except that I have red hair instead of her beautiful jet-black), I've certainly never felt I could step into her shoes. I've never managed to help Frankie the way Mom always did.

"We're done," I called to Dad as we came back into the house.

Frankie said nothing. He just gathered Neelia up in his arms and went straight to his bedroom.

I found Dad in the kitchen making Christmas dinner. Dad is a fantastic cook! He has always been the one who puts dinners together, even when Mom was with us. She used to joke that we'd have had to rely on frozen dinners, takeout pizza, and popcorn (her favorite snack) if she'd had to do the cooking!

As I climbed up on the stool by the kitchen island to watch, I said, "Dad, I'm really worried about Frankie. It will break his heart to lose Neelia."

Dad sighed and nodded. "I know. But you know what, Ginni? Life is strange sometimes. As I told Frankie, it makes no sense that Neelia doesn't belong to someone. But life doesn't always make sense, either. We are going to do everything possible to find her previous owner. But I have a strange feeling about Neelia. I can't put it into words, but it seems she belongs here.

"But remember this: I've learned that worrying never helps. What does help is believing. So, let's believe Neelia will end up where she is meant to be. Now, help me by setting the table for our Christmas dinner."

As I walked around the dining room table laying out plates, glasses, and silverware, I couldn't get Dad's words out of my head. 'Believing,' huh? That was fine for things like the Tooth Fairy and the Easter Bunny, but this was Frankie's heartbreak and a real-life kitten we were talking about. How could simply *believing* help? I grew even more skeptical as my mind shifted to the night before when Dad had called the barn owl by his scientific name, *Tyto furcata*. Now, how could a scientist take comfort in simply believing? That didn't make sense. And I knew he, too, already had feelings for Neelia. But who was I to argue with Dad? I decided to start thinking positive thoughts and to believe that Neelia was here to stay.

We had just sat down to dive into the Christmas ham when Neelia started making a fuss. At first, I thought she wanted to sit on Frankie's lap during dinner—which I knew Dad would never allow.

But I was wrong.

Neelia pawed at the empty chair and meowed her heart out. We all stared at each other, just as we had when Alexa had played "White Christmas" the night before.

I froze, fork halfway to my mouth. That was Mom's chair. No one had used it since she died. But now, Neelia seemed to think it was hers.

First the lights had turned on and off, then Alexa had played "White Christmas," and then Tyto had led us outside to find a lost kitten. And now Neelia wanted to sit in Mom's chair. Did Neelia have some sort of connection to Mom? Was that why Neelia's fur was the color of Mom's black hair? Or why Mom's favorite color was the color of Neelia's collar? Was it possible Mom had sent her to us? I shook my head. No way. That wasn't possible. That would take Dad's 'believing' conversation a bit too far!

I was sure Dad would brush Neelia away and we'd just go back to dinner, but he surprised me. He got

up, walked over to the chair, and pulled it out. Neelia jumped up, landed light as a feather, and sat tall. Dad didn't even scold Frankie when he placed a small amount of Christmas ham on his salad plate and gave it to Neelia.

I was trying very hard to believe, but whatever would we do if Neelia had to go?

CHAPTER THREE

WHO'S THE CULPRIT?

The next day was Friday, with one week of Christmas break down and one more to go. Frankie and I were playing his new board game on the dining room table, and Dad had just made the call to Little Paws Clinic, the veterinarian's office. He'd arranged an appointment with Dr. Little for Neelia on Monday.

Shortly after the phone call, he shouted from the kitchen, "Where's your Grandma Hollister's teaspoon? I was just using it!" Dad walked into the dining room, hands on hips, with a quizzical look on his face. "That's the third item that's gone missing since you guys have been on break, and your mom would never forgive me if I misplaced her mom's favorite teaspoon!" he moaned.

"First, when I was wrapping your mom's special snowflake earrings that I was giving to you, Ginni, I had found a perfect small bow to go on the package. I stepped away for a minute, and it was gone when I got back. Yesterday, I never did find your mom's Air Force wings I was going to take to the jeweler. And now, I turn my back to get baking soda for the chocolate chip cookies I'm making, and Grandma Hollister's teaspoon that I had laid on the counter is gone. Which one of you is the culprit?"

Frankie and I looked at one another, wide-eyed. Now, I could usually tell when Frankie felt guilty about something, but there wasn't an ounce of guilt on his face—and I knew I hadn't taken any of the items. We looked back at Dad, and both of us shook our heads.

"Well, if neither of you has been taking my things, are you suggesting I'm losing my mind?" said Dad with a bit of a twinkle in his eye.

"Well, Dad, you know, your 40th birthday is coming up," I teased.

Dad grinned, shook his head, and went back to the kitchen.

A few minutes later, Dad's cell phone rang, and he yelled that it was for me. I took the phone and went up to my bedroom to answer the call, while Frankie and Neelia trailed behind me.

"Hey, Ginni," said my friend Catherine on the other end. "You guys want to go sledding at Totem Trails Park on Sunday morning? We're supposed to get a big snowstorm on Saturday night. Plus, I want to hear all about what you got for Christmas."

"Oh, Catherine!" I rejoiced. "I can't wait to fill you in on what's been going on over here during break. Yes! Let's go sledding on Sunday morning. I miss you!"

Catherine, Sharnelle, and Rose are the three girls who live in the house next door with their mom, Ann Pebbles. They moved in about three years ago from Jamaica, and Catherine has been my best friend ever since. I love visiting their house. Ms. Pebbles has decorated it as if the house were sitting on a Caribbean Island. And I enjoy hearing the stories of what life was like for them when they lived in Jamaica.

After I finished our conversation, I bounded into Frankie's room.

"Catherine just told me it's supposed to snow tomorrow night—a lot. She invited us to go sledding early Sunday morning. Doesn't that sound like fun?" I asked.

"Sure," said Frankie. But I could tell he was distracted. "Ginni," he said, "you're not going to believe this."

"What is it?" I replied.

"I can't find the origami cat I made last night. I left it right on my bookcase when I went to bed, and now it's not there," Frankie reported. Mom had been teaching Frankie origami techniques, and he was getting very good at it.

Then it dawned on me. "Frankie, I didn't think about this until right now, but when I went to work on my embroidery last night before bed, I couldn't find my favorite thimble—the one Mom gave me on my birthday last year. It seems Dad's not the only one missing things!"

That's when I started twirling a few strands of my hair.

"Oh no," cried Frankie, "not the hair twirling!"

I laughed. Whenever there is a mystery to solve, I have a habit of twirling a few strands of hair around my finger. I guess it makes me feel like Nancy Drew. "Frankie, I believe we have a mystery!"

"Oh, boy!" Frankie exclaimed.

While Neelia jostled in Frankie's arms, we rushed down the curved staircase and raced into the kitchen to find Dad.

"Dad," I cried, "we have a mystery!"

Dad looked up from his iPad, his missing items obviously forgotten. "Say what?" he asked.

"You said you have had several things go missing, right?" I asked.

"Yes," replied Dad.

"Frankie just told me the origami cat he made last night is missing, *and* I'm missing my favorite thimble! It's not only you who's missing things."

"Well, it sounds like a mystery, indeed!" Dad said. "What are we going to do?" Dad was always so frustratingly practical.

"I don't know," I said. "What do you suggest?"

"I suggest we all watch and wait," replied Dad. "The culprit will make a mistake and reveal him- or herself— that's my guess."

Just as he said this, Neelia jumped from Frankie's arms and raced out of the kitchen.

The three of us followed.

Neelia was now prowling and sniffing throughout the living room. She was crouched on her belly and was inching her way toward the staircase. Then she bounded up the stairs.

"What's gotten into Neelia?" Dad asked.

"I'll go find her," Frankie said, racing up the stairs.

Dad and I stood in the living room, dumbstruck. First, we had all the mysterious things happening, and now it seemed we had a thief among us. Could the thief be Neelia?

"Dad, you don't think it's Neelia taking these things, do you?" I asked.

"Well, except for the small bow for your present, Ginni, Neelia has been with us all the other times," Dad said. "We should probably keep a very close eye on her. We wouldn't want her to choke on anything."

Just then, Frankie came back downstairs, carrying Neelia.

"When I got up there, she was sitting on my bed like a princess," he reported.

Dad explained to Frankie that we needed to supervise Neelia to make sure she wasn't playing with items that wouldn't be safe for her.

When Dad said that, Frankie—worried about Neelia's safety—hugged her so tightly I thought she'd squawk. But she didn't. Instead, she licked Frankie's cheek, as if to assure him she'd be just fine.

"How about we take Neelia back upstairs, and let's see about getting your sewing machine set up, Ginni," Dad suggested.

The big grin on my face was all the answer Dad needed.

When we got to the upstairs landing, Dad said, "Before we go into Ginni's room, Frankie, why don't you show me where your origami cat was sitting the last time you remember seeing it?"

Once in his room, Frankie pointed to a shelf on his curved bookcase. "I had it right here," he said. "It was a black cat."

"No surprise there," Dad laughed—it was a perfect example of his dry humor.

We left Frankie's room, and Dad asked me where I

had kept the thimble that was now missing.

"I was working on an embroidery project before Christmas, and I had laid it on the side table, along with the needle and embroidery floss," I told Dad.

"Hmm," was all Dad said.

"What are you thinking?" I asked.

"Well, it seems as if all the items—Frankie's, yours, and mine—were out and easily accessible. Wouldn't take much for someone or something to sneak away with them," Dad said. "I repeat, we had all better keep a close eye on Neelia, just to make sure she doesn't get herself into trouble." With that, Frankie settled on my bed, holding Neelia protectively.

Dad and I took my new sewing machine out of the box. It was so shiny, I felt as if it should just sit on display!

"You know, Ginni," Dad said, "your mom and I should have gotten you a small sewing table to set this on. How about if, for now, we use your side table? Before break is over, we'll go shopping and see if we can find an appropriate sewing table."

"Can't argue with that, Dad," I said with a huge smile. I cleared my handiwork off the side table, and Dad and I moved it in front of the window.

"You'll need good lighting to see all those intricate stitches this machine will make for you, Ginni," Dad said.

With Frankie petting Neelia and Dad setting my new sewing machine on the table, only one thing could have made me happier: if Mom could have been with us. Now it was up to me to learn how to thread my machine on my own and get it ready to go. Mom and I would have had so much fun doing this together.

Neelia must have sensed my thoughts, for she left Frankie on the bed and came over to me, pawing my legs to be picked up. While holding her could never replace having Mom with us, it was surprising how much comfort she brought to me just when I needed it.

Share Joy

CHAPTER FOUR

WE ♥ PETS

I had just gotten up the following morning, enjoying the sun glistening off the snowy rooftops, when I heard Dad calling.

"Frankie," Dad yelled from the back entryway.

"Coming," Frankie yelled back as he slid down the staircase.

Dad handed Frankie some money and said, "You'd better make a trip to the pet store and purchase a real litter box and some cat litter for Neelia. I don't think she's very happy with the cardboard box and gravel we set up for her on Christmas Eve."

Frankie's face immediately started to glow.

"Say, now, this doesn't mean anything permanent, Frankie," cautioned Dad. "I just think Neelia is getting disgusted with doing her duty in gravel."

Frankie took the money, saying, "I know, but it'll be fun to buy her something, at least."

"Well, don't get carried away," said Dad. "Just the litter box and a small bag of litter—anything else will have to wait. And you'd better take Ginni; you might need some help to carry the litter back."

Fifteen minutes later, Frankie and I were bundled in our winter jackets and hats and were heading out the front door. I could hardly keep Frankie from skipping down the street. He was so happy!

"Frankie, you heard what Dad said. This doesn't mean she's staying," I warned. But my heart wasn't in the warning. I loved seeing Frankie act like his carefree, loving self again.

"Oh, I know," Frankie replied.

I simply sighed and let him be happy. The truth was, we all needed a little happiness right then, and his was contagious. I even started skipping right beside him. I probably was too old to be skipping with my younger brother, but at that moment I didn't care. It was good to feel happy.

But when we got to the pet store, my good mood sank. There, propped up against the storefront, was Stanley's mountain bike.

Stanley lives next door and is in my class. He can be pretty mean. Dad says he is lonely, and we should try to be friends with him, but Stanley's behavior makes that hard to do.

For example, I'll never forgive Stanley for what he said to Frankie and me on our first day back to school last fall. Frankie and I both enjoy school, and the first day back is usually full of excitement and wonder for what the upcoming year will hold. But last fall, it had been the first day back after losing Mom over the summer. I wondered how all my friends would react to me, and what Frankie's friends would say and do.

Stanley started it off by catching the two of us as we turned the corner to walk up the entry sidewalk. "Hey, you two," he shouted, "what's it feel like to be an orphan?

"Oh, that's right," he continued. "You're not completely orphaned . . . you still have your dad alive, don't ya? I guess you're only half-orphans!" He jogged away, all the while laughing to himself.

My only consolations were that no one else was close enough to hear his hurtful comments and that Frankie really wasn't paying attention—he was still lost in his heartbreak. Also, after that incident, Stanley never again called us 'half-orphans.' I wondered why. Could it be that even he realized he had gone too far?

As we entered the pet store, I heard Stanley sneer, "Well, if it isn't Carrot Top and Baby Brother."

Frankie immediately stopped in his tracks and inched closer to my side.

"What are you doing here, Stanley?" I asked, ignoring the taunt.

"Just hanging," Stanley replied. "Seeing if I can get a reaction from some of the mangy animals in here."

Stanley took a stick from his pocket and started banging on the cats' cages, which sent them all into a tizzy.

"Stop that!" Frankie yelled.

"Who's going to make me? You, Baby Brother?" Stanley laughed.

"Stop calling me that!" Frankie said with all the bluster he could manage.

I was about to step in when the salesclerk intervened. "Young man," she said calmly, "it's time for you to leave."

"Humph!" Stanley retorted. "You've got nothin' but some sick old barn cats anyway. I'm outta here."

"Thank you," I said to the salesclerk after Stanley left.

"Oh, you're welcome," she said, "but it's the cats I was worried about. They are already stressed at having to wait here until they find their forever homes; they don't need to be treated like that. Now, what can I help the two of you with today?"

I explained that we had found a kitten on Christmas Eve. I thought about telling the clerk all the strange things that had happened with Neelia's showing up at our house, but I thought she wouldn't believe me. I decided then and there that I should probably share Neelia's story with only our most trusted friends. But I did tell the clerk that we were waiting for the vet to open on Monday to see if she had a microchip, and that if she didn't, we hoped we'd be able to keep her. "If we do keep her, we'll be back to buy a bunch of cat toys," I said. "But in the meantime, we just need a small litter box and litter."

"I have just the thing," the clerk said as she led us to the litter aisle. "Here's what many people use when they take their cats traveling."

It was a small yet serviceable plastic domed litter box that even had a purple carrying handle.

"That'll be perfect," I said as Frankie grabbed it and headed to the checkout counter.

"And some litter?" the clerk reminded us.

"Yes," Frankie called back. "I almost forgot."

"Here's a perfect size for the litter pan," said the clerk as she handed me the litter. "You know, every cat needs toys, so here are a couple of chasing toys you can have—on the house—while you wait to hear from the vet. Even if she's with you only a couple of days, she deserves to play."

"Thank you," I said. "Neelia loves to play, and I'm sure she'll have fun chasing these." But what I really was thinking was that *Frankie* would love having some real cat toys in order to properly play with Neelia.

We paid for the purchases and began the walk home. Frankie carried the litter box while I hefted the bag of litter. Frankie had obviously gotten over the Stanley encounter and happily swung the litter box by its purple handle, all the while describing how he and Neelia would play hide-and-seek with the new cat toys.

"We're home," Frankie hollered as we walked in the door. "You still want the litter box by the back door?"

"Sure," said Dad, calling out from his office. "I'll be right there to help you."

I followed Frankie to the back entryway and set the litter down for him. "I'll make sure Dad doesn't get caught up on something so he can help you," I told Frankie. But what I really wanted to do was to catch Dad before he left his office so I could update him on what had happened with Stanley. I never did tell Dad about the 'half-orphan' comment; it was just too painful. But I usually let him know the things Stanley does. Then maybe Dad will think twice about encouraging us to be friends with him.

"Dad, just so you know, Stanley did it again. He was at the pet store when we got there. He called us some names and then took a stick and started banging on the cats' cages. It made me so mad!"

"What happened then?" asked Dad.

"The nice salesclerk came over and told him to leave. Stanley even called those sweet kitties 'mangy barn cats'!"

Dad laughed. "Well, I'm glad to see you're more upset about what he called the cats than what he called you! Shows me your heart's in the right place."

I giggled at that, but it wasn't the reaction from Dad that I had hoped for. He and Mom always forgave people so easily. This was another way Mom and I differed. Maybe someday I can be more like her. I'm just not sure Stanley will ever be someone I can forgive.

By the time we both got to the back entryway, Frankie had emptied the litter into the box, and Neelia was looking it over.

"Let's give the little girl some privacy to check out her new commode," suggested Dad.

As we walked toward the living room, Frankie was talking Dad's ear off about all the cat accessories we'd have to get once Neelia was ours.

"Oh, I almost forgot," I said. "The salesclerk gave us some cat toys for free. She said even if Neelia is only with us a few days, she still deserves to play."

"Hmm," was all Dad said.

Just at that moment, Neelia walked in. Frankie tossed one of her new toys, and she immediately bounded after it. It was game on after that! Frankie would toss it, Neelia would chase it, and then Frankie would toss a different toy. They both kept scurrying around the living room, and it was impossible to tell whether Frankie or Neelia was having more fun.

Again, Dad had this huge grin on his face, and I could tell that he was falling more and more under Neelia's spell. Could I cross my fingers and hope any harder we'd get to keep her?

That evening, as Frankie and I were getting ready for bed, Frankie knocked on my bedroom door. I put down my book and went to see what he wanted.

"Ginni, you'll never guess," said Frankie as he stood barefoot in the doorway.

"What?" I asked.

"I went down to get Neelia's toys and bring them to my room, and the purple ball is missing," he reported.

"Well, I'm sure Neelia just knocked it out of sight under the couch or something while the two of you were playing," I said. "Don't worry about it. Even if she did steal it, it's a cat toy and safe for her to have."

Frankie felt comforted by what I told him—hey, maybe I was getting to be a bit more like Mom after all!

But although I told Frankie it probably had gotten knocked under something, that wasn't what I believed. Something in my gut told me the cat toy was an additional item to add to the Missing Items list.

Frankie went back to his room, and I settled into my bed after I turned off the battery-operated tealight candle I usually have on at night. I wondered when the culprit was going to make a mistake, like Dad had said, so we could find out who or what it was. But maybe there was more to do than simply wait.

Maybe, I thought, we should set a trap.

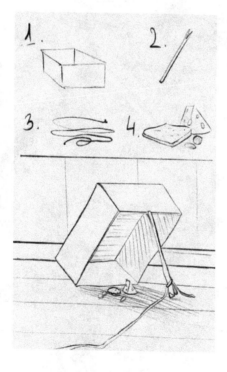

I drifted off to sleep, unconsciously twirling a few strands of my hair.

CHAPTER FIVE

SNOWY MORNING

I woke up Sunday morning to a blanket of fresh snow covering the lawn, trees, and rooftops. Everything sparkled. Catherine's weather prediction had come true. It really had snowed a lot last night!

As I bounded down the stairs, I could hear Frankie and Dad talking in the kitchen.

"You two are up early," I said with a yawn.

"Yes," cried Frankie. "Are we still going sledding with the girls today?"

"I'm pretty sure we're still on, but Dad, will you text their mom to check while I go upstairs to get ready?"

"Sure," answered Dad. "Anything for a day of peace and quiet around here to watch some football games!"

When I got back to my bedroom, I did a little dance. There is something magical about new snow, and I was excited to spend the day outside with friends.

Dad called up the stairs and told me we were to meet the Pebbles girls at nine o'clock in the driveway. "Are you sure you don't want me to drive you and the sleds to the park?" he asked.

"Let me check." I turned toward my Alexa and said, "Alexa, what's the temperature outside?"

In her standard pleasant voice, Alexa announced, "It's 41 degrees and sunny."

"Nah, we can walk. It's not far," I called back to him.

When I got downstairs, Dad was helping Frankie get everything packed.

"I put a backpack together with some trail mix, a couple of sandwiches, and a thermos of hot cocoa," Dad said, zipping up Frankie's jacket.

"Did you put in enough for the girls?" I asked.

"No. I actually got the idea from Ann. She's making sandwiches for them. I thought you guys had better have something to eat as well," said Dad. Ms. Pebbles always has such good ideas. She is also a nurse, which often comes in handy around here.

"Can we take Neelia?" pleaded Frankie.

"Son, we have no idea if Neelia would like being outside that long in the cold, or if she would stay close to you. It's not worth the risk, now, is it?" Dad asked.

"Yeah, you're right, Dad," sighed Frankie.

"Besides, I like the idea of having a football buddy!" laughed Dad, petting Neelia. "Now, you'd better get going. I see the girls are heading out."

Just as we met up with Catherine, Sharnelle, and Rose, a light snow began to fall. This was going to be a special day!

I turned my head back to the house to wave goodbye to Dad, and I saw Stanley standing in his front picture window. The garage door was open, and I noticed neither of his parents' cars were parked inside. It looked as if Stanley was the only one home. I guessed this went to support Dad's comment that Stanley was perhaps lonely. He seemed to be home alone a lot. Maybe I was imagining it, because I was a ways away, but I would

have sworn he looked envious. If only he weren't such a bully, he could have joined us. Geesh! Was I beginning to think like Mom and trying to forgive him for all the mean things he'd said? For a split second, I thought maybe we should invite Stanley, but then I shook my head—*I'm not that forgiving yet,* I told myself. *Who wants to be tormented all day?* I turned back to my friends, doing my best to forget about Stanley.

After spending almost all of our time at home with Neelia since Christmas Eve, it felt good to chat with the girls. Frankie couldn't stop talking about Neelia and how special she was.

Catherine is one year older than I, and I have always looked up to her. Sharnelle is one year younger, and Rose and Frankie are both seven. The ages of us all are so close, it's no wonder we get along really well. Catherine and I fell back in step and let the younger kids walk ahead of us. This was my time to fill her in on the details of Neelia and how devastated we all would be if we couldn't keep her.

"Catherine, I have a story to tell you that you're going to find hard to believe. I've been waiting until we were together to share with you exactly what's been going on since Christmas Eve. I don't trust anyone other than you and your family to share this with," I said.

"Gee, can you build up the suspense any higher?" laughed Catherine. "What's going on?"

"Obviously, getting through Christmas this year was tough," I began. "And we were all going through the motions of Christmas Eve, having a steak dinner, lighting candles, opening presents, all our usual stuff. But of course, it wasn't—and never will be—the same without Mom. There was one present left to open, mine, when strange things started happening."

"What things?" asked Catherine. I could tell she was curious.

As I told Catherine about all the weird things that had happened Christmas Eve, her eyes got wider with each event.

"No way," she exclaimed when I told her about Alexa playing "White Christmas."

"You've got to be kidding," she said when I explained Tyto's flying around the house and knocking on the door with his beak.

I looked directly at Catherine after her comment, and she and I shared a moment with both of us looking deep into each other's eyes, the way only best friends can do. I was starting to get a bit nervous about sharing all of this with her. What if she didn't believe me? What if she thought I was telling her this only to get attention? Would I lose my best friend's trust?

But I guess not, because she seemed intrigued and nodded her head, prompting me to continue.

That's when I told her about Tyto's flying to our maple tree, leading Frankie to run outside and find a little black kitten huddled in the snow.

Catherine's eyes lit up when I mentioned the kitten. Ever since second grade, Catherine has wanted to be a veterinarian. Her house is always full of animals: hamsters, white rats, hedgehogs, you name it!

"Was the kitten okay? Was it hurt at all?" Catherine asked.

I had to smile to myself—yep, Catherine was going to grow up and become a vet; I just knew it in my heart.

"The kitten was fine," I reported. "And, surprisingly, Dad let us bring it into the house. He looked it over, and we've had her ever since."

"That sounds great," Catherine exclaimed. "I bet Frankie loves her."

"You have no idea, Catherine," I told her. "Frankie and the kitten have already bonded—in fact, the whole family has fallen in love with her.

"But now the sad news," I continued. "On Christmas Day, Dad made Frankie and me post 'Found: Kitten' signs all around downtown. See, the kitten has a collar with a name tag. The name printed on her tag is Neelia. With that collar and name tag, she must belong to someone."

"I can see why you're worried," Catherine said gently. "Watching Frankie with Sharnelle and Rose, I've never seen him so excited—especially since your mom died."

I gave Catherine a quick hug. I knew I could count on her to understand just how much Neelia had come to mean to Frankie and the rest of us.

I finished my story by telling her the coincidences of Neelia's black fur and Mom's hair, and Mom's favorite color being the color of Neelia's collar right before we got to the park. I didn't share our culprit mystery with her though. That story could wait until another time.

But I did tell her that Mom had bought me a sewing

machine right before she died. It had been the present waiting for me once we got Neelia into the house. Catherine knows how much I love sewing and crafts. She gave me another hug, saying, "You know, your mom would be very proud of you for how much you're helping your family. You're the woman of the house now."

Catherine's words gave me a great deal to think about as we entered Totem Trails Park. The woman of the house! Was I up for that? I guessed I had no choice *but* to be. It seemed like a big responsibility, though. What does the woman of the house do? Before I could think about it anymore, Catherine urged me on towards the sledding hill.

Totem Trails Park is an incredible place. Like our town, Makawee, the park was named to honor Native Americans. There are several historical plaques and statues in the park telling the story of the Native American tribes who used to live there. The park is also full of fun things to do. It has awesome playground equipment (complete with a curly slide), walking trails, a river, fireplaces with huge chimneys, and, best of all, a great hill for sledding.

The fresh snow made for perfect sledding conditions, and we were the first ones there to break in new runs. We were having a blast!

I was about to tell Catherine I was surprised no one had beat us to the sledding hill when it dawned on me: Catherine hadn't planned this sledding date just because we were about to get a huge snowfall. She'd planned it so we would have something special to do today.

SNOWY MORNING

I had forgotten all about that day's annual Snow Carnival at school. Every spring, the fifth graders go on an overnight camping trip to a local campground. They need to raise money to help cover the cost. So the fifth-grade parents put on a carnival for the entire school during Christmas break. It's always a good time. You can catch up with your friends and share what you got for Christmas. There are plenty of carnival games to play, and they bring in pizza, cotton candy, and all sorts of great food. Best of all, there is a book fair.

On our walk home from school the last day before Christmas break, I had told Catherine that Frankie and I had both decided to skip the carnival this year. Things had settled down with my classmates, but at the carnival, kids from all grade levels would mingle. I know most of them are just trying to help, but with kids I don't see very often, they always feel they have to ask how I'm doing without Mom.

I want to scream back at them, "How do you think I'm doing? It stinks! It's unfair! And I've finally stopped crying myself to sleep every night!" But, of course, I can't say that. So I just mumble, "It's getting better," and walk away.

I couldn't stand the thought of an entire day at the carnival, seeing so many different kids and being questioned all afternoon. So, enter my savior, Catherine, who set up a special sledding day for something else to do. She and her sisters had given up the Snow Carnival for us. I had to brush away a tear as I realized what she had done.

That was why we were the only kids there that morning! *Duh!*

I don't know how many turns we took as we raced down the hill, but it was getting to be sandwich time. I was at the top of the hill, and Frankie had just headed down one more time when I went to get the backpack. I stopped dead in my tracks when I heard Frankie scream, and my stomach dropped to my knees.

I looked down the hill, and there he was, lying on his side, holding his foot. Sharnelle and Rose were at the bottom of the hill and were already on their way to Frankie as Catherine and I raced downhill as fast as we could.

As soon as I got down there, I could see what had happened. Buried in the snow was a huge rock. Frankie must have jammed his foot against it on his trip down.

"Can you move it?" I asked as I very gently unlaced and pulled off his boot.

Frankie tried but grimaced with every wiggle of his toes.

Since it wasn't even noon yet, everyone was at the carnival, and we were still the only ones on the hill. How was I going to get Frankie home?

At that moment, a barn owl swooped over our heads. I looked up just in time to see it head back into town.

"Did you see that?" I yelled. Was that Tyto? If so, what was he doing here?

The girls and I watched the barn owl for a second, but then Catherine and I each took one of Frankie's arms and started to walk him up the hill. It was very slow going. Frankie couldn't put any weight on his bad foot, and it was hard to help him hop up the steep hill.

We had just gotten to the top when I saw Dad pull into the parking lot. How had he known to come to the park? He jumped out of the car and ran to us.

"What happened?" asked Dad as he took Frankie out from under Catherine's and my arms.

As he gently lifted Frankie into the car, we all started telling the story at once.

"The hill was perfect for sledding," I began.

"We were about to break for a bite to eat," continued Rose.

"The hill was so fast!" interjected Sharnelle.

"Wait, wait, wait!" laughed Dad. "I can't listen to you all at once. Ginni, tell me what happened."

"Well, as Sharnelle mentioned, the hill was slick, and the new snow had covered everything," I said. "Frankie was on his last trip down before we were going to get something to eat when I heard him shout in pain.

"There he was," I continued sadly, "at the bottom of the hill holding his foot. He had run into the side of a huge rock. I know it must have been buried under the fresh snow, for when he hit it, I could see he had knocked some of the snow off the rock. He was holding his foot, and I knew he shouldn't walk on it, so Catherine and I carried him so he wouldn't put any weight on his injured foot.

"But how did you know we needed you to come to the park, Dad?" I asked.

"Let's just say for now that a little birdie told me," said Dad, shrugging off my question. "Everybody else okay?"

"Yep," I answered. "Frankie's the only casualty."

"Very funny," Frankie retorted.

Dad told us to load everything into the car for the drive home.

"Can you move your toes?" Dad asked Frankie. When he found out he could, he decided to drive us home instead of to the hospital. "We'll ask our next-door nurse to stop over and take a look."

Ms. Pebbles came right over, carefully examined Frankie's foot, and assured us it was just a sprain.

"Say, will you look at that," said Dad right after Ms. Pebbles left.

"What?" Frankie and I asked in unison.

"Before I left for the park, I was just about to enjoy a big bowl of popcorn when Neelia jumped at me, and I spilled about a cup of popcorn on the floor. I didn't get a chance to pick any of it up. Look at what's left."

Dad hadn't made popcorn since Mom died. We used to have it for our Sunday night snack almost every week. Was this evidence of Neelia's lifting Dad's spirits like she had Frankie's?

There on the floor beside Dad's chair were about three kernels of popcorn—certainly not a cup's worth.

"I'll add it to our Missing Items list," I sighed. "You know, since you took Neelia with you in the car to the park, she couldn't have been the popcorn thief!"

"You're right, Ginni," Dad replied. "Guess we have to keep investigating."

So much had been going on, I hadn't even had time to think about how to trap our thief. But this was getting serious. I would have to start creating a plan.

After Frankie was settled in Dad's recliner with a huge ice pack on his ankle, I finally had time to ask Dad again about something that was still bothering me. "So tell me, Dad, how did you know to come to the park?"

"I don't think you're going to believe me," Dad started, "but Neelia and I were having a great time watching the 49ers beat up on the Cowboys when all of a sudden she jumped from my lap. I thought maybe she needed to use the litter box or something, but instead she found one of my winter gloves and brought it to me. Then she started meowing something awful. After that, she tugged at my pant leg.

"I couldn't figure out what she wanted until she went to the door, scratching at it as if she wanted to go out. She's never done that since she's been here. That's when it dawned on me—something might have happened to you kids. So I took a chance, grabbed Neelia, put her in a box so she'd be safe, tossed her in the car, and off we went. And I'm glad I did. You guys would never have been able to limp Frankie all the way back home."

SNOWY MORNING

As if it weren't going to be hard enough to let Neelia go if we found her previous owner . . . we now had a Rescue Cat!

CHAPTER SIX

DR. LITTLE

By Monday morning, Frankie's ankle was almost as good as new. He still walked gingerly on it, but it was feeling better since Dad had wrapped it in an Ace bandage.

Dad surprised us mid-morning by announcing he was going to take us to the Village Diner for lunch before we went to the vet. The four of us had always enjoyed grabbing a bite to eat at the diner, but we hadn't been there yet without Mom.

I felt like dressing up a bit more than the various sweats I had been wearing all week—after, all, we were going out to lunch! I put on my best jeans and the fisherman's sweater Mom had knitted for me. The snowflake earrings Dad gave me for Christmas would look great with the sweater. I got dressed and went to my nightstand, where I keep a small tray for my favorite earrings. My heart sank. Only one of the snowflake earrings was in the tray!

"On no," I cried. "My Christmas present from Dad is now on the Missing Items list!"

Well, I wouldn't tell him—not right away, at least. But we really needed to find the culprit!

I changed sweaters to my red-and-black cardigan. I knew I was being silly, but the snowflake earrings would have been perfect with the fisherman's sweater, and I didn't want Dad to wonder why I wasn't wearing them. I didn't think he'd really notice, but I thought it was better to be safe than sorry.

When we got to the restaurant, our usual booth was occupied, so we had to sit at a different table. It was probably for the best. I never knew how frequently everyday life activities can cause pain when someone you love is gone. I could almost hear Mom saying, "You can't live sheltered in your home; you have to go out and live your life." I guess it was time to start making new memories.

Chelsea, our favorite waitress, was on duty, and she immediately came over to help us, already carrying a tray with our drinks. I was waiting for a comment such as, "So nice to see you back again! How are you all doing?" But thankfully, she just greeted us as normal. "What can I get you guys for lunch today?" was all she asked.

I ordered a hamburger with ketchup, pickles, and onions—just the way Mom liked her burgers—while Frankie had his usual chicken nugget meal, and Dad rounded out our order with a chef salad.

When Dad got up to pay the bill, I saw an older woman at the next table eyeing Dad as he walked to the cash register. This was not uncommon. Mom always teased Dad about how women seemed to fawn over him with his 'chiseled good looks.' Even the elderly ladies on our block give him great big smiles. Mom often commented that he was lucky to still have all of his wavy brown hair. Like Frankie, Dad has blue eyes, and Frankie and I both got our angel kisses from Dad's side of the family. I grinned to myself, wondering if Frankie would be as good-looking when he got to be Dad's age.

After Dad came back to our table, I checked my watch and announced, "We're too early for our appointment at the vet's office, Dad."

"Yes, I know," he answered, "but we have a couple of errands to run first."

Frankie and I looked at each other. Usually Dad wasn't so secretive. He was a list guy. Normally, we headed out with a checklist of errands with the routes all planned to avoid any backtracking.

We followed Dad out of the diner, down the sidewalk and around the corner. Dad was taking us straight to Treehouse Crafts.

The coolest part of Treehouse Crafts is the fake tree in the back corner with a small treehouse in it for the little kids. I remember sitting in the treehouse when I was younger, looking over the many craft books while Mom was shopping. They even have coloring books, simple punch cards kids can sew together with shoestrings, and other easy crafts. Being small for my age, I can still fit into the treehouse, although I won't be able to much longer.

I looked up at Dad with a questioning look in my eyes.

"You need a sewing table, right?" he asked.

I had almost forgotten that he'd promised to buy a real sewing table for me. I enthusiastically nodded as we walked into one of my favorite stores.

And here it was, another first for the day. I hadn't been in the craft store since Mom died either. Wow! What a day moving forward I was having.

We went to the back corner of the store, where all the sewing supplies were, and I immediately found a perfect table. It was just the right size. I didn't have a lot of space in my bedroom for a huge table. This one was compact, yet it had all the compartments needed to store bobbins, needles, thread, and other sewing notions.

My eyes opened wide when I looked at the price tag. I was about to tell Dad we could just keep the sewing machine on my side table, when I heard him telling the clerk this was the table we wanted.

"The floor model is all we have right now," the clerk explained, "but I'd be happy to deliver the table to you as soon as it arrives. We are expecting a shipment from our supplier any day."

"That'll be perfect," said Dad, and he went to the front to make arrangements.

My fingers trailed along the bolts of fabric as we slowly walked out of the store. I was imagining all the fun I'd have sewing. I may not have truly known what the word *bittersweet* meant before Mom died, but I sure do now. It was so fun to be setting up my own sewing station, yet it was so heartbreaking to be doing it without Mom. Time to make new memories, I guess.

"Is it time to walk home and get Neelia for the vet?" asked Frankie.

"Not yet," answered Dad. "We still have one more stop to make."

Frankie and I looked at each other. I was glad I wasn't the only one noticing that Dad was acting differently today.

We stepped out of Tree House Crafts following Dad as we walked right past my favorite store, Sunshine Books. *Guess Frankie and I don't get to pick out any books today,* I thought. But if that wasn't where we were going, I couldn't imagine where it would be.

We passed Sweet Georgina's Chocolate Shoppe as well. *No sweets today, either,* I thought. Right next to the chocolate shop was a cell phone store, and to my surprise, that was where Dad led us.

All this fuss over Dad's going into the cell phone store to pay his bill? I pondered. *Gee, what a production!*

The three of us ambled into the store, and Frankie and I went to look at the cool stuff they had on display while we waited for Dad to go to the counter and pay his bill.

It was about a minute before Dad joined us at the display rack with a salesclerk in tow.

"This is my daughter," Dad told the clerk, "and the new phone is for her."

"Really?" I gasped. I leapt into Dad's arms and gave him a huge hug.

"Yesterday's incident on the sledding hill told me it's time for my little girl to have her own cell phone," he said. "We can't keep relying solely on a Rescue Cat!

"Now, of course, there will be rules and stipulations on the phone, you know," Dad warned. "No spending all your free time texting or talking to Catherine and your other friends. And there will be other conditions." But I didn't care. I was so happy to know I'd be getting my own cell phone!

"Gee, Frankie, when I need a new computer, you'll just have to break your arm!" I teased. Frankie just glared at me.

"Now is it time to go back and get Neelia?" asked Frankie after the clerk helped us get my new phone activated and ready to go.

Frankie had been very patient at the craft store and while I was getting my phone, but I could see that the stress of getting to the vet and finding out whether Neelia was microchipped or not was wearing on him.

"Yes," said Dad, "let's swing by the house and pick up Neelia."

Usually, Frankie and I both had a hard time keeping up with Dad on walks because of Dad's long legs, but now Frankie was on a mission. Even with Frankie's sore ankle, I had to power walk to keep up with the two of them on our way back to the house.

Neelia met us at the door, and Dad placed her in the box he'd used when he came to get us at Totem Trails Park. He had improved it by adding airholes and a towel for her to lie on.

"It's my homemade cat carrier," he said. "What do you think?"

"It's great, Dad," I replied.

Neelia obediently lay down in the box, almost as if she knew she was going out. Frankie ran to the craft box and grabbed a black marker. When he returned, he wrote NEELIA on the side of the box. We closed the top and took off.

Carrying a cat in a box is not as easy as you might think. All Neelia had to do was shift a bit in the box, and it threw off the entire balance of the load.

"Hmm," said Dad as he struggled to keep Neelia balanced. "I guess I didn't think about how the box would work when Neelia moved inside."

We giggled as we watched Dad shift the box around as we trekked to the vet. It took us quite a bit longer to get to the vet carrying Neelia than it had to race back to the house to get her, but we still managed to arrive at the vet's on time.

During the entire walk, I was doing my best to 'believe,' as Dad had told me four days ago when we were getting ready for Christmas dinner. But to be honest, I had never been so scared in all my life. The best thing I could do, I knew, was not to show Frankie how scared I was. That would only have made him all the more worried. When we opened the door to Little Paws Clinic, all I could say to myself was, *This is it. Believe!*

"Well, is this the little black kitten I've seen on the signs posted all around downtown?" asked Dr. Little as we stepped into the exam room.

"Yep, she is," said Dad.

"She's even cuter in person," said Dr. Little, smiling as he gently lifted Neelia out of the makeshift cat carrier.

"Dr. Little," said Frankie, "we really want to keep her. Please don't find a chip."

"I understand completely, Frankie," Dr. Little said kindly. "But let's start by giving her a checkup and make sure she's as healthy as she looks."

Dr. Little took out his stethoscope and listened to her chest and tummy. He weighed her, peeled back her lips to look over her teeth, shone a light into her eyes and ears, and even put a thermometer up her butt!

"Dr. Little," Frankie exclaimed, "can't you just hold it in her mouth?"

Both Dr. Little and Dad laughed. "Wish I could, Frankie," Dr. Little said, "but look, it's already over."

After the thermometer, I could have sworn Neelia had a woozy look on her face.

Then Dr. Little handed Dad a small brown bag. "Jim, this duty is for you," he told Dad.

"You need to collect a stool sample for me."

Now Dad looked woozy!

"Don't worry," said Dr. Little. "All the directions are in the bag. Piece of cake!"

"Easy for you to say," mumbled Dad under his breath.

We had never had a pet before, but we have known Dr.

Little for a long time. Since both he and Dad work downtown, they know each other as fellow business owners. They frequently eat lunch together at the diner, and they even golf together on occasion. And Dr. Little often stops by the house for a variety of reasons. But this was the first time I had seen Dr. Little being a vet. What kindness and care he was showing Neelia! This was a man I could trust.

"Believe." I must have said it out loud, because everyone in the exam room looked at me.

"What did you say, Ginni?" asked Dad.

"Nothing," I said with a little cough, trying to disguise my comment. I felt embarrassed, but since no one had really heard exactly what I said, I didn't have to explain myself.

"Oh, I almost forgot," said Dr. Little. "Let's look to see if she has a microchip."

"Let's not," Frankie whispered.

Dr. Little left the room and came back with a big wand-like instrument and ran it over Neelia. "Hmm," he said.

"What?" cried Frankie.

"Well, I agreed with your dad, Frankie," said Dr. Little. "You would think such a cute, well-behaved kitten like this one, with a collar and name tag, would have a chip, but I see no indication of one."

I didn't know whether Frankie was going to jump up and down for joy or faint. I think he did a little of both!

"Hold on," Dr. Little cautioned. "Don't get too excited yet. The law says you have to wait five days for an original owner to claim a lost pet before you can adopt it. And my advice is to start the five-day count now, not on the day you put up the signs. With so many people gone over the holidays, you want to give them a chance to get back home and see your signs."

"Five days!" whined Frankie.

"Yes," said Dr. Little. "But even after that, you as a family will need to decide what you're going to do if, a month or two from now, some boy or girl knocks on the door and claims her. Your actions will help you grow into the person you want to become," advised Dr. Little.

While the fact that Neelia didn't have a microchip was the best news ever, I had never thought we'd have to wait five more days to adopt her. And it had never crossed my mind about someone stopping by the house days or weeks or even months later, trying to claim her. How would Frankie handle the stress? How would I? How would someone prove Neelia had been theirs? This was another time I wished Mom were here to provide us with her words of wisdom.

Dad told us to wait at the vet's while he went back home to get the car. I guessed he didn't want to struggle with the box again. Ten minutes later, he picked us up, and we hopped into the car.

I was in the front seat with Dad as we drove home. Frankie and Neelia cuddled in the back. As we walked into the house, I could see Neelia's black fur was wet. Frankie had been crying.

Mom, I pleaded silently, *please help everything work out.* I rarely talked to Mom, but if ever we needed some extra help from heaven, it was now.

CHAPTER SEVEN

THE FIVE-DAY WAIT

So, the waiting began.

Day 1: No news.

Day 2: No news.

Day 3: One phone call, but the caller said her missing kitten had white feet—whew, not Neelia.

Day 4: No news.

Day 5: No news.

After dinner on Day 5, the four of us sat down in the living room to watch *The Secret Life of Pets*. Neelia was curled up on Frankie's lap. I knew Frankie was dying to talk to Dad. We had made it through five days, and no one had claimed Neelia. But I also knew Frankie dreaded the discussion about someone claiming her in the near future.

The movie had just started when Neelia bounded off Frankie's lap. Dad paused the show as we stopped to watch Neelia.

Then we heard what had caught Neelia's attention. There was a rustling noise, and the Christmas tree skirt moved!

Neelia pounced!

The Christmas tree skirt went flying as Neelia chased underneath. We heard squeaks and meows—and then more squeaks and more meows—until Neelia came out from under the wadded-up tree skirt with a mouse in her mouth!

We all stood up, amazed at what was happening before us.

I turned and pressed my head into Dad's chest; I knew what cats did with mice, and I didn't want to see it.

But instead of hearing Frankie cry out in horror, I heard him giggle! What kind of person would giggle over a cat eating a mouse? Curiosity got the better of me, and when I turned my head to look, there was Neelia, licking the little mouse from head to tail.

Soon the two began chasing each other around the tree and playfully batting at one another. "Well, I'll be!" was all Dad could say.

"Guess we got to the bottom of your mystery, Ginni," said Dad as he lifted the rumpled Christmas tree skirt.

There, hidden under the red skirt, were all the missing items.

"You little culprit!" I exclaimed. "Guess I won't have to come up with a trap after all. Looks like Neelia solved the Culprit Mystery!"

"You know what, kids? We have a pretty small house. If we keep adding to our little family like this, one of you is going to have to sleep in a closet!" Dad teased with a wide grin. "Ginni, grab your phone and text Catherine to see if they have a cage, mouse food, and other items we'll need to get the little guy settled for tonight," said Dad.

I couldn't believe Dad was so agreeable to keeping another pet.

"Really, Dad?" I asked. "You're going to let us keep him?"

"Well, it looks like Neelia and this little guy are already friends. We can't break up a friendship!" Dad answered.

I grabbed my phone and sent the text to Catherine. In no time at all, she arrived at the front door with a cage, bedding, a hamster ball, and a bag of mouse food.

"How did you end up with a mouse for a pet?" she asked.

It was time to tell her about our Culprit Mystery. So, very quickly, I mentioned that over break, all of us had been having small items of ours go missing. At first we'd thought it might be Neelia. However, Neelia had solved the mystery when she heard rustling under the Christmas tree skirt and captured a mouse. I pointed to the tree skirt, which still had the items lying around it.

Catherine laughed at our little mystery. "These are all extra supplies we had, and they're yours," she said. "Can I see the little guy?"

We had let the mouse crawl into a small box while we were waiting for Catherine to arrive. She took the box, placed it on the floor, and knelt to peer inside.

"Look at those long whiskers!" Catherine exclaimed.

"That's it, Catherine!" I cried. "I've been trying to think of a name for the little guy, and you nailed it! We'll call him Mr. Whiskers!"

"You know, we could call him *Mus musculus*," teased Dad.

"Enough with the scientific names, Dad," I laughed back. "Mr. Whiskers is a much cuter name!"

Just then, along came Neelia and started batting at Mr. Whiskers. Catherine gasped, but I calmly said, "Just watch."

And then Neelia continued chasing him with her paw while Mr. Whiskers bobbed back and forth.

Pretty soon, Neelia leaned down into the box, and the two of them nuzzled.

"Well, I'll be," was all Catherine could say.

"You might want to write a paper on these two someday for one of your veterinarian classes," Dad laughingly told her.

"I just might, at that," answered Catherine. "Well, I can't stay. We were just about to sit down to play Monopoly when you texted. I should get back. Oh, and by the way, thank you, Dr. Pearl, for getting Ginni her own cell phone. Now I don't have to bug you when I need to contact her."

Dad opened his mouth to say something, but Catherine stopped him.

"I know what you're going to say," she laughed. "Don't worry, we both will be careful not to overuse our phones!"

As we shut the door behind Catherine, I took the supplies to the couch and carefully placed a small amount of bedding in the cage. I knew we'd get more stuff for Mr. Whiskers, but for now, this would work.

The cage even had a little exercise wheel in it.

In a matter of minutes, we were back on the couch, Neelia on Frankie's lap, Mr. Whiskers in his cage on my lap, and Dad sitting between us.

Dad picked up the remote, and we settled in to finish watching our movie.

When the credits came up, Dad shut off the movie and said, "Well, Frankie, I think you should buy some more cat toys and food tomorrow. And Ginni, you'd better go along and pick up some items for Mr. Whiskers as well."

Frankie leapt up, surprising Neelia, and she fell off his lap. Frankie hugged Dad with tears streaming down his face.

With his arms tightly wrapped around Dad's neck, he whispered, "But what if someone claims her later?"

"You tell me, Son," Dad said gently.

"Well . . ." Frankie could hardly get the words out. "If someone shows up, and if Neelia is truly theirs, then she'll have to go back."

"Frankie, that is the most adult decision you've ever made. I am so proud to call you my son."

And then Dad took us both into his arms with a huge, loving hug.

This Christmas was definitely going to be one to remember. Although Neelia had finally solved the Culprit Mystery, we still had bigger mysteries on our hands. What about the connections between Neelia and Mom? And how were Mr. Whiskers, Tyto, and Neelia connected? Would we ever solve these mysteries? Maybe not.

And had Mom sent Neelia to us? Could that even be possible? How would I ever know? But just in case she had, I raised my eyes to heaven and sent Mom a thank you.

"Mom," I said, "I love you, and I will miss you every day of my life. But I know we learned how to believe, live life and move forward, thanks to Neelia. Thank you for sending us the kitten who saved Christmas."

COMING UP...

Be sure to follow Ginni, Frankie, Neelia, Tyto, and Mr. Whiskers on their next adventure, *The Kitten Who Cured a Grump*.

Georgina, the owner of Sweet Georgina's Chocolate Shoppe, is usually the happiest person in town. Who wouldn't be when you're surrounded by yummy chocolate every day?

So why is Georgina suddenly grumpy and downright mean? And why is the Chocolate Shoppe closed in the middle of the day?

And what's the strange noise Ginni keeps hearing?

Find out in Neelia's next adventure.

ACKNOWLEDGMENTS

Thanks to Jim, for without his gentle push (or was it a kick in the butt?), this book would never have been written.

I also want to acknowledge my team at DartFrog. Thanks for helping me hone and shape my story into a book that I am truly proud to present.

And most of all, to my sister. Thank you for your support and encouragement, not only for *Vine Street Mysteries* but throughout my entire life. You have always been in my corner, and because of this I have been able to reach for the stars.

ABOUT THE AUTHOR

Nova DuBois has spent her life among children's books and elementary-aged children. She began her love of children's literature in her early teens when volunteering at her hometown's library where she held Saturday morning storytelling hour and assisted in maintaining the children's book area. This passion resulted in pre- and post-graduate degrees in library science. She enjoys bringing stories to life for children and watching their imaginations soar.

She has her own special black cat who helps provide inspiration for the *Vine Street Mysteries* series. This is the first book of this series, and who knows where her black cat will lead her?

CPSIA information can be obtained
at www.ICGtesting.com
Printed in the USA
BVHW090807090322
630946BV00006BA/19